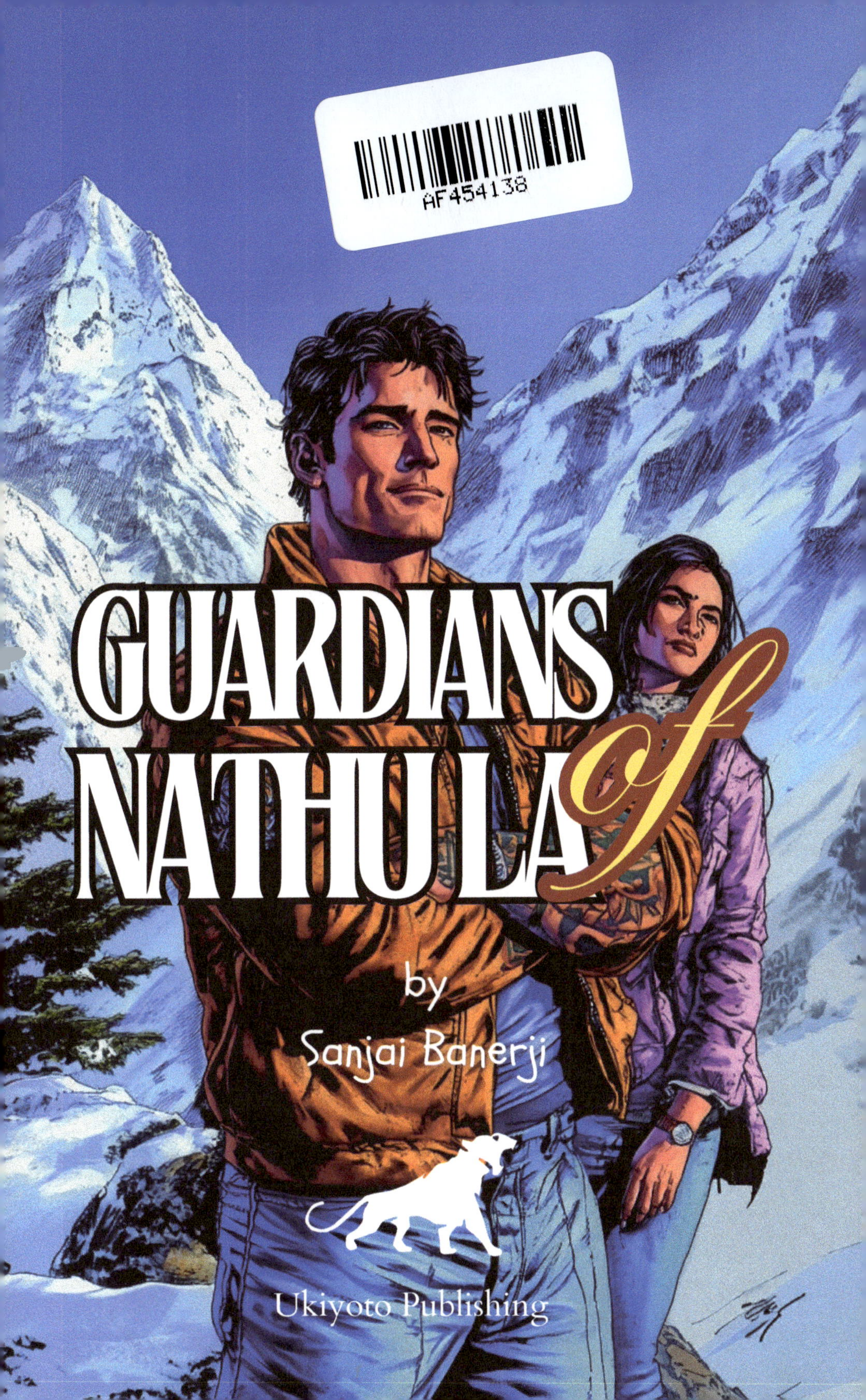

AF454138
GUARDIANS of NATHU LA
by
Sanjai Banerji
Ukiyoto Publishing

The driver at the wheel of the Scorpio halted at the Nathu La Army Camp.

Manisha was very excited, as any eight-year-old would be.

The vehicle was part of a convoy of tourists that had arrived at Nathu La Pass from Gangtok. The tourists arrived at Nathu La and spent three hours along the Indo-China border, strangely divided by just a yellow nylon rope.

Manisha visited the Army Tourist Center with her Aunt, from where they received a certificate for seeing Nathu La Pass with an authenticated stamp and signature of an army officer.

Manisha got herself photographed with her Aunt at the 'Memorial Wall of Brave Soldiers,' who had lost their lives.

An army canteen served Maggi Noodles and soup with bread. A funny incident happened. A young man sat opposite Manisha's Nathu La Army Canteen table, eating noodles. There was also a cup of coffee on the table. He wore a red and black checkered-sleeved shirt unrolled at the elbow, displaying a tiger tattoo on the left arm.

The eyes of the tiger caught her attention. The pupils were blue. Manisha surmised that although the tiger appeared frightening, the blue eyes removed the evil from the face of the tiger. She was so enamored by the tattoo that she caught the eyes of the man, who moved his left arm resting on the table towards her. He smiled at her, and Manisha smiled back. Manisha earnestly wanted to look at the tattoo and got up from her chair.

Timi kahām̐ jādai chau?
Hoin, Hoin Basa.
Ma tattoo herna cahanchu.

Suddenly, the man on the opposite side with the checkered shirt approached them.

Yes. That's true. I understand Nepali. My mother is a Gorkha.
Good afternoon, Sir. Sorry. I think you overheard our conversation in Nepali.
But tell me, Mr. Mukherjee, the tiger looks scary. What does it signify?
That's a nice-looking tattoo.

Two of the most common meanings associated with the tiger tattoo are power and strength. In nature, the tiger is the top predator in its environment. Therefore, a tiger tattoo can represent a free spirit or independence. Along with these positive connotations, the tiger can symbolize danger, vengeance, or punishment. Fortunately, my tiger tattoo has blue eyes, which signifies a good tiger. Strong and reliable.

Wow. That's one helluva tiger! My name is Junali Rai. I am Manisha's paternal Aunt from Pedong near Kalimpong in West Bengal. I can understand some Bengali too. "Kamon Accho?"
Khub Bhalo.

Manisha and her Aunt were in the convoy of Scorpio vehicles 6th in line and behind Mobius's vehicle. While returning from Nathu La Pass, the tourist convoy stopped at the shrine of the late Baba Harbhajan Singh of the 23rd Punjab Regiment, who died at the borders in 1968, a year after being posted at the Indo-Chinese border in Sikkim.

By 3 pm, the convoy descended from the shrine when disaster struck. It was an avalanche. The landslide of boulders started suddenly, and there was chaos all over.

Their vehicle was trapped between two giant boulders. Manisha could see behind them all the vehicles retreating fast. In front, the vehicle in which Mobius was traveling sped away, leaving them stranded. Manisha watched with dread as she saw more boulders coming from the mountainside. The vehicle driver and her Aunt looked at each other in trepidation. The foreboding of evil loomed large on the trio.

As Manisha got down from the Scorpio, she realized the height of the boulder obstructed her view, and there was no way she could know what was happening behind it. Her Aunt was also desperately moving around because the boulders were tightly wedged on sides, front and back. Suddenly, the checkered shirt man's head loomed from behind the boulders.

Manisha's face bobbed. Mobius caught her in his arms and gently
lowered her to the ground. Next came Tunali.

The driver was a hardy Pahadi, small in stature but with a very flexible body. With a single leap, he scrambled up the boulder and was down at the other side, even before Mobius could put Junali on her feet.

Mobius instructed all three of them to start running. Mobius's vehicle was a hundred meters in front. The small-built driver beside Mobius sprinted ahead. Mobius urged Junali and Manisha to run as fast as possible.

Mobius looked at the mountainside. At the slow pace they were moving, the rolling boulders would undoubtedly hit them. He had to make a quick decision. Mobius knelt on the ground.

While running, Mobius felt the strain of a 60-kilogram woman pulling him back and simultaneously running with a 20-kilogram child. The boulders were crashing down at an alarming rate. It was touch and go, Mobius thought to himself.

As Mobius fell to the ground, he took the precaution to pull Junali beside him and twisted around to touch the ground heavily on his back, holding Manisha close to his chest. Mobius bore the brunt of Junali and Manisha on top of him, protecting them and taking his breath away with the impact.

A giant boulder almost brushed Mobius's shoes; such was the momentum of the big stone, which continued its path down below after bouncing twice on the gravel path.

After a moment, Mobius looked sideways. Suhail was kneeling on the ground, muttering, with eyes closed as if silently praying. Manisha, though not appearing to be hurt, had begun crying.

Mobius felt too weak to get up. Suddenly, they were surrounded by soldiers in battle fatigues. They were the Indo-Tibetan Border Security Force. Mobius could feel several hands lifting him gently from the ground. He was being carried to a nearby army ambulance. It then struck him about the whereabouts of Manisha and her Aunt. A voice loomed on top of him.

This is Major Bakshi. You are now in safe hands. Your group is coming with you, so don't worry. I shall follow the ambulance in a jeep to our military hospital ten kilometers away.
Mobius felt too weak to get up. Suddenly, they were surrounded by soldiers in battle fatigues. They were the Indo-Tibetan Border Security Force. Mobius could feel several hands lifting him gently from the ground. He was being carried to a nearby army ambulance. It then struck him about the whereabouts of Manisha and her Aunt. A voice loomed on top of him.

Once the Ambulance started with all three inside, Junali stood beside Mobius who was in a stretcher.

The ambulance ground to a halt after an agonizing half an hour for Mobius outside the Military Hospital, where army hospital staff took Mobius down on the stretcher.

With relief, Mobius got off the stretcher, stretched himself, and felt his back. The shirt was torn at the back. There were some raw wounds, and Mobius, after feeling them with his fingers, realized soon after that his fingers were blood-stained.

Major Bakshi escorted them to the surgical ward in the hospital, where his shirt was removed and wounds cleaned, disinfected, and bandaged. Junali had some abrasions on both her elbows, which were disinfected. The entire procedure at the Surgery took about an hour.

Good news, Mr. Mukherjee, your ruck-sack was handed over to us by your driver. I have also instructed my jawans to salvage your friends' belongings from the vehicle and bring them to me. I am taking you, the lady and the girl, to stay the night at our home on the hospital campus. The rest of the tourists were accommodated in the Army barracks, and both men and women were segregated. Below 10-year-olds stay with their mothers.
The ever-smiling Major Rakshi was waiting outside the Surgery

Major Bakshi, we are already much obliged for what you have done for us. We can stay in the barracks.

No way, Mr. Mukherjee. My jawans and I watched your death-defying hundred-meter sprint with your friends. You saved the lady and child from imminent death by pulling them across to safety. My wife and I will be honored to have you all as our esteemed guests.
OK, Major. We most certainly can't refuse the honor.
Right then, young man, after you.
Major indicated Junali and Manisha to follow Mobius as he walked aside from Manisha.

The dinner was early, at 7 pm. The kind Major, taking advantage of Mobius's raw wounds, spoke to his superior officer and arranged to have an Ambulance pick up Mobius and the group and drop them off at their respective Hotels in Darjeeling. In the bedroom, Mobius took charge after Junali and Manisha had a bath, and Mobius sponged himself due to the dressing on his back.

Let's get our maths right. Junali, you are four years older than I am at 25. I'll call you Junali. You can call me Mobius.
I can't be your father because you are eight. Hence, Manisha, you are my younger sister, and I call you Manisha or Kanchi.
That's cool.
And I shall call you Baagh Bhai, which means Tiger Brother.

OK, fine. Now I sleep on the sofa, and both of you in the bed.
Oh, come of it, Mobius. The bed is big enough for the three of us. Your legs will dangle on the sofa.
I will manage.
OK, we need to talk a bit.
Not yet. What about you, Junali?
Mobius. Are you married?
I am unmarried, living with Manisha's parents in Pedong. I have a small store selling grocery items with Manisha's mother. Before I forget, here's our telephone number. I have it on a piece of paper.

Is that your girlfriend's photo? She is beautiful. She looks like a sportsperson like you.
Yes, she represented Uttar Pradesh in badminton and volleyball in the under-nineteen team. She did her post-grad in English from Delhi University.
Wow, what credentials! You are one lucky man, Mobius.
Mobius put the paper safely in his wallet. As he flipped his wallet open, Junali saw a photo of Sumitra.

Mobius got up from bed and dug himself on the sofa. He was fast asleep in five minutes.

The Major's wife had prepared their packed breakfast of tomato and egg sandwiches with a thermos of tea. The ambulance was parked in front of the Major's home.
The orderly in the ambulance was a portly 30-year-old who claimed to be a palmist before he joined the Army.

Look at our palms and tell us something.

Isn't that poetic rhetoric?

This girl is the enlightened one. She is going to be a leader of people. She is destined to become very famous. She will lead her community to the very pinnacle of accomplishment and prominence.

No, Sir, it is not. Her head and fate lines are solid. Furthermore, her index and middle fingers are well-developed in thickness and length. The long index finger suggests leadership and the long straight middle finger points to trustworthiness and responsibility.

The orderly looked at Manisha's hand as he spoke.

Now tell me about myself.
Anything wrong?
Sure, Sir. Show me your right palm..
No, Sir, but you need to play your cards right. Your life is going to be very complicated. You appear to get in and out of trouble. But there is good news. Your wife will be powerful. Your wife will love and protect you to the hilt of a dagger. She will be your guardian. I see, Sir, you have a tiger tattoo on your left arm.
Becoming very interested, Mobius rose and sat closer to the orderly. The orderly spent a few minutes pondering

The orderly looked at the tattoo for some time.

Mobius, I will help you since you need to leave for Bagdogra immediately.
Thanks, Junali. That will be a big help.
The three reached their Hotel at 11:30 am.

Mobius's cab had already arrived and was waiting on the hotel porch. It was a hurried farewell for Mobius.

Mobius hugged Manisha and shook hands with Junali.